MID-CONTINENT PUBLIC LIBRARY
15616 E. 24 HWY.
INDEPENDENCE, MO 64050

D1310648

WITHDRAWN
FROM THE RECORDS OF
MID-CONTINENT PUBLIC LIBRARY

Ernest & Rebecca

4

"The Land of Walking Stones"

Guillaume Bianco – Writer

Antonello Dalena – Artist

Cecilia Giumento – Colorist

PAPERCUTZ
New York

To my love Susanna
   -Antonello

A big thanks to Barbara Canepa for her generous help and
to Florent Bonnin for his availability and helping hand!
   -Guillaume

Daddy

He's an artist. A painter...
like Picasso, but better!
We have lots of fun together
when mommy's at work...
He's the funniest daddy
of all!

Mommy

She's the most beautiful
mommy of all! She's not
at home a lot because of
her job, but she always
finds time to cook my favorite
food for me: "steak and
fries with ketchup and
mayonnaise!"

Coralie

She's my big sister.
I adore her, even if,
ever since she's been in
her rebellious stage,
she stays in her room
all the time.

Ernest

He's a microbe...
and he's my best friend!
I caught him one day
while on a frog hunt.
Since then, we're
always together... He's
super smart and really
strong: he can change
into anything!

And me: Rebecca!

I'm not very big...
It's 'cause I hate soup!
I'd rather eat ketchup
and chase frogs with
Ernest in the rain!

Sam

He's my mom's fiancé.
He's nice, but I'm suspicious
he's really some kind of
evil germ trying to
contaminate our family unit.

Ernest & Rebecca
graphic novels
available from
PAPERCUTZ

Graphic Novel #1
"My Best Friend is a Germ"

Graphic Novel #2
"Sam the Repulsive"

Graphic Novel #3
"Grandpa Bug"

Graphic Novel #4
"The Land of Walking St

ERNEST & REBECCA graphic novels are available at booksellers everywhere. Or order online from www.papercutz.com. Or call 1-800-886-1
Monday through Fridays, 9-5 EST MC, Visa, and AmEx accepted. Available in hardcover only, #1 & #2 are $11.99 each, #3 and #4 on are $10.99
To order by mail, please add $4.00 for postage and handling for first book ordered, $1.00 for each additional book and make check payable to N
Publishing. Send to: Papercutz, 160 Broadway, Suite 700, East Wing, New York, NY 10038.

Ernest & Rebecca
#4 "The Land of Walking Stones"

Guillaume Bianco – Writer
Antonello Dalena – Artist
Cecilia Giumento – Colorist
Jean-Luc Deglin – Original Design
Florent Bonnin – Colorist, pages 34 & 35
Joe Johnson – Translation
Janice Chiang – Lettering
Michael Petranek – Associate Editor

Jim Salicrup
Editor-in-Chief

© DALENA – BIANCO – ÉDITIONS DU LOMBA
(DARGAUD-LOMBARD S.A.) 2012
www.lombard.com
All rights reserved.
English Translation and other editorial matter
Copyright © 2012 by Papercutz
ISBN: 978-1-59707-400-1

Printed in China
March 2013 by New Era Printing LTD.
Unit C, 8/F Worldwide Centre
123 Chung Tau St, Kowloon, Hong Kong

Distributed by Macmillan
First Papercutz Printing

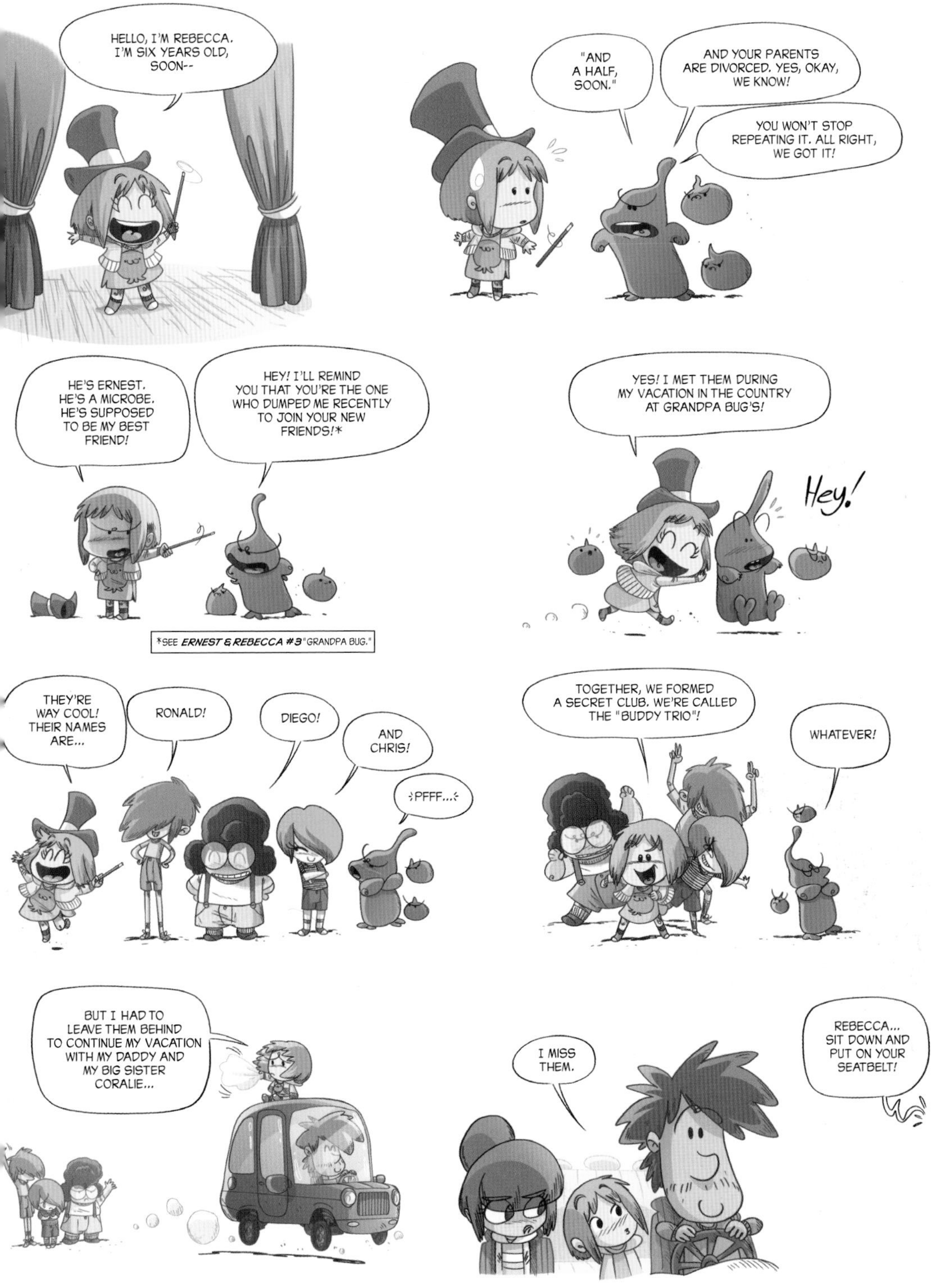
HELLO, I'M REBECCA. I'M SIX YEARS OLD, SOON--
"AND A HALF, SOON."
AND YOUR PARENTS ARE DIVORCED. YES, OKAY, WE KNOW!
YOU WON'T STOP REPEATING IT. ALL RIGHT, WE GOT IT!
HE'S ERNEST. HE'S A MICROBE. HE'S SUPPOSED TO BE MY BEST FRIEND!
HEY! I'LL REMIND YOU THAT YOU'RE THE ONE WHO DUMPED ME RECENTLY TO JOIN YOUR NEW FRIENDS!*
*SEE ERNEST & REBECCA #3 "GRANDPA BUG."
YES! I MET THEM DURING MY VACATION IN THE COUNTRY AT GRANDPA BUG'S!
Hey!
THEY'RE WAY COOL! THEIR NAMES ARE...
RONALD!
DIEGO!
AND CHRIS!
PFFF...
TOGETHER, WE FORMED A SECRET CLUB. WE'RE CALLED THE "BUDDY TRIO"!
WHATEVER!
BUT I HAD TO LEAVE THEM BEHIND TO CONTINUE MY VACATION WITH MY DADDY AND MY BIG SISTER CORALIE...
I MISS THEM.
REBECCA... SIT DOWN AND PUT ON YOUR SEATBELT!

...AND DON'T PUT YOUR FEET ON THE WINDOW PLEASE...

WHEN WILL WE GET THERE?

WE LEFT BARELY THREE HOURS AGO, SWEETIE.

I'M HOT.

WE'RE GOING TO TRY TO NOT TURN ON THE AC, OTHERWISE YOU'LL GET SICK...

I'M THIRSTY. I WANT SOME GRENADINE.

DON'T DRINK TOO MUCH. YOU'LL GET SICK TO YOUR STOMACH...

HERE!

SO, WHERE ARE WE GOING? ⸓GULP!⸓ ⸓GULP!⸓ ⸓GULP!⸓

I'VE ALRE TOLD YO A HUNDRED T SWEETIE

"TO THE LAND OF WALKING STONES"!

YEAH, BUT WE'RE NOT GOING VERY FAST! EVERYBODY'S STOPPED ON THE HIGHWAY!

⸓GULP!⸓ ⸓GULP!⸓

STOP WITH THE GRENADINE. YOU'VE DRUNK ENOUGH!

DADDY?

YES, SWEETIE?

I'M SICK TO MY STOMACH...

WE'LL STOP AT THE NEXT REST AREA.

IN THE MEANTIME, TAKE THIS PAIL, YOU NEVER KNOW...

BUT WHY ARE YOU GIVING ME THIS PAIL, CORALIE?

WELL, IN CASE YOU WANT TO THROW UP...

BUT... BUT... I DON'T WANT TO THROW UP!

THAT'S GROSS!

I TOLD YOU NOT TO DRINK SO MUCH GRENADINE!

BUT YOU ALWAYS DO AS YOU PLEASE!

REATHE, IT'LL PASS.

HELLO.

GRENADINE, GRENADINE...

GRENADIIIIIIIIIIINE...

GRENADINE, GRENADINE!

DADDY!

GRENADINE...

I THINK I'VE CAUGHT THE PUKING BUG... ⋅SIGH.⋅

THERE... IT'LL PASS DON'T WORRY...

BREATHE IN DEEP... LIKE THAT...

EXHALE...

INHALE...

WE'LL WAIT FOR YO... THE CAR, OKAY?

YES, CORALIE.

THANKS...

INHALE...

EXHA--

PERSPERATION!

IT STINKS OF PERSPER--

SMELL OF PERSPIRATION!

STOP!

DOG POOP!

PEEPEE SMELL!

SPINACH!

I CAN... HEAR Y...

UPCHUCKED SAUERKRAUT IN SOCK JUICE!

YOU WON'T MAKE ME THROW UP!

TOEJAM UNDER YOUR TOENAILS!

YUCK...

THAT'S ENOUGH, OR I'LL CALL ERNEST! AND HE'LL GIVE YOU A GOOD WHIPPING!

ER... ERNEST?

AHAAAAA! NOT SO CLEVER NOW, EH? I KNOW HIM REALLY WELL, HE'S MY FRIEND. HE'S SUPER STRONG, SO WATCH YOUR BUTT!

ERNEST? THE MICROBE WHO EATS SLIMY SNOT FROM SICKLY KIDS, SLURPING IT IN LIKE SPAGHETTI?

≥BUH-LARFF!≤

SHE GOT IT ALL OVER HERSELF. WE'LL HAVE TO STOP AT A SERVICE STATION...

VACATIC... OFF TO A START...

SOME WHAT?

SOME MEDICINE FOR A SICK STOMACH, PLEASE.

BUT UH, THERE'S NO SUCH THING...!

YOU'RE BEING STUPID! THERE IS SUCH A THING, I'M SURE THERE IS!

HERE, TAKE ALL OF MY SAVINGS!

GIVE ME YOUR BEST MEDICINE!

AH, WHY YES! IT'S COMING BACK TO ME! I MUST HAVE IT SOMEWHERE, MISSY!

ERE, LITTLE LADY! THE "MIRACLE MEDICINE"!

IT'S A MAGICAL BAND-AID!

WHAT DO YOU SAY, HONEY?

ANK YOU, SIR!

DID YOU SEE, DADDY? THE SALESMAN IS SO COOL! HE TOLD ME THAT, BY PUTTING IT ON MY NOSE...

I WOULD NEVER GET QUEASY AGAIN, HA HA HA!

DADDY, HE WOULDN'T E BEEN PULLING MY LEG, WOULD HE?

UH, NO, COME NOW... WHAT AN IDEA...

IT'S A USED BAND-AID... THERE'S NOTHING MAGIC ABOUT IT... IT WAS ON THE BIG TOE OF THAT FAT, HAIRY MAN'S STINKY, SWEATY FOOT...

BLAAAARRFFF....!

AND THERE! WE'RE FINALLY LEAVING THE HIGHWAY AND NONE TOO SOON!

HAS YOUR SISTER FALLEN ASLEEP?

IT SURE LOOKS LIKE IT...

GOOD!

AND YOU, SWEETIE, NOT TOO TIRED?

YOU CAN SLEEP A BIT IF YOU LIKE...

NO, IT'S OKAY... I'M NOT SLEEPY.

YOU'RE MISSING YOUR SWEETHEART FREDDY STEVENS, AREN'T YOU?

⸸PFF⸸, HE'S NOT MY SWEETHEART, FOR STARTERS! I DON'T CARE ABOUT HIM...

AND I DON'T WANT TO TALK ABOUT IT EITHER.

YOU KNOW, YOU DON'T HAVE TO COME WITH US. IF YOU WANT TO GO BACK AND S HIM, I CAN DROP YOU OFF AT THE NEX TOWN'S TRAIN STATION.

WHAT DO YOU SAY?

IT'S ALL RIGHT, I SAID!

OKAY... AS YOU WISH...

AND HOW ARE THINGS AT HOME?

ANY WORD FROM YOUR MOM?

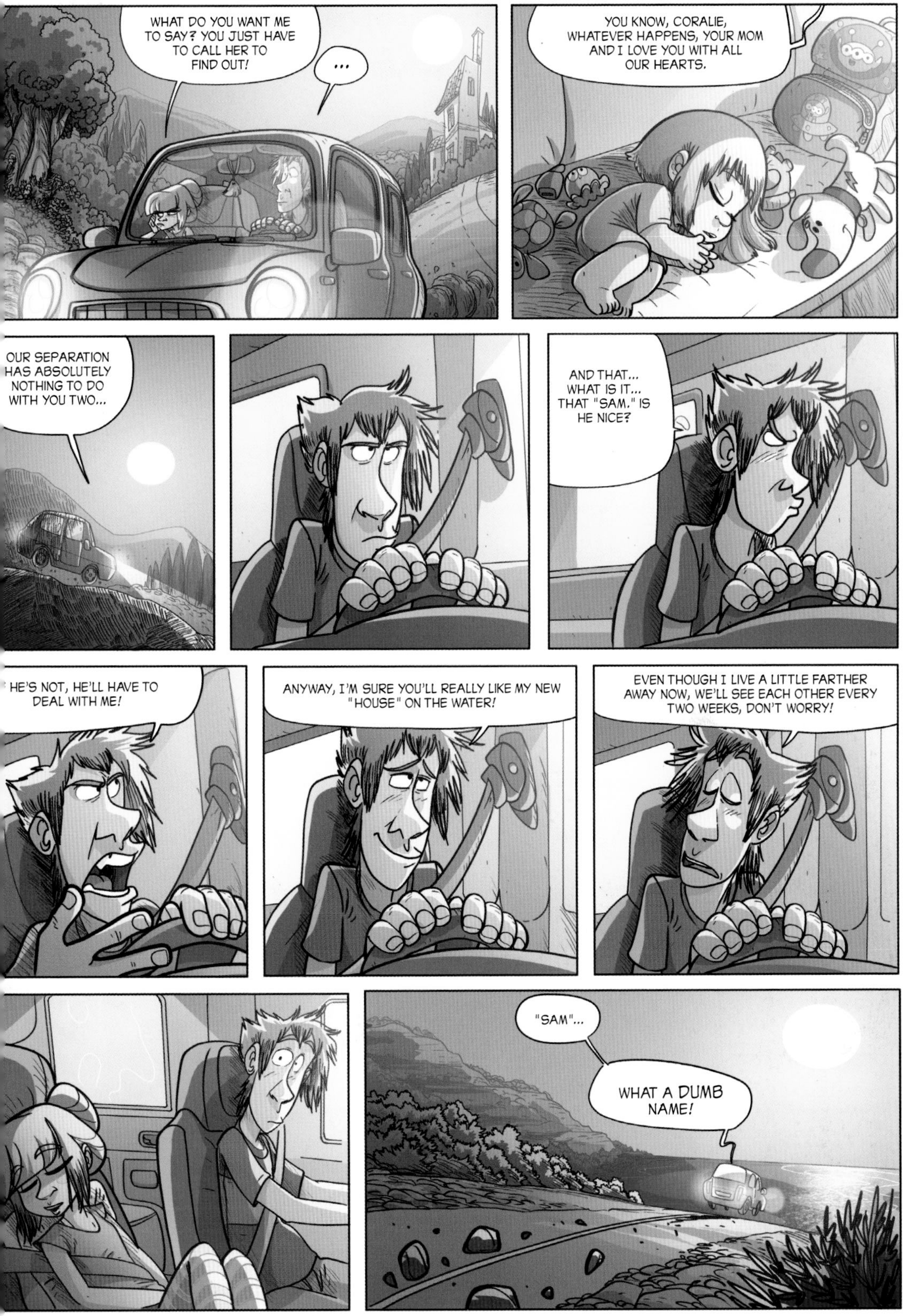
WHAT DO YOU WANT ME TO SAY? YOU JUST HAVE TO CALL HER TO FIND OUT!
...
YOU KNOW, CORALIE, WHATEVER HAPPENS, YOUR MOM AND I LOVE YOU WITH ALL OUR HEARTS.
OUR SEPARATION HAS ABSOLUTELY NOTHING TO DO WITH YOU TWO...
AND THAT... WHAT IS IT... THAT "SAM." IS HE NICE?
HE'S NOT, HE'LL HAVE TO DEAL WITH ME!
ANYWAY, I'M SURE YOU'LL REALLY LIKE MY NEW "HOUSE" ON THE WATER!
EVEN THOUGH I LIVE A LITTLE FARTHER AWAY NOW, WE'LL SEE EACH OTHER EVERY TWO WEEKS, DON'T WORRY!
"SAM"...
WHAT A DUMB NAME!

DADDY FINALLY DID MAKE A DETOUR...

ON THE TRAIN PLATFORM, I WAS STILL A LITTLE BIT ASLEEP, BLEARY-EYED WITH DROWSINESS...

I WASN'T AWARE IF IT WAS REAL LATE OR REAL EARLY...

WHICHEVER IT WAS, IT WAS STILL DARK WHEN CORALIE'S TRAIN LEFT...

SHE SEEMED HAPPY TO BE GOING HOME TO MEET HER DEAR FREDDY STEVENS...

NOT HESITATING ONE SECOND TO ABANDON DADDY AND ME...

BUT I'M NOT REALLY MAD AT HER. DEEP DOWN, I THINK I UNDERSTAND HER...

ONCE THEY GET TO A CERTAIN AGE, BIG SISTERS DON'T LIKE GOING ON VACATION ANY MORE WITH THEIR FAMILY...

CHRIS, THE "BUDDY TRIO," MISSILE...

...GRANDPA BUG, GRANNY DOODLE, AND MY BEST FRIEND ERNEST AREN'T AROUND ANYMORE...

SO, HERE I AM TRULY ALONE ON VACATION WITH MY DADDY...

WANT TO TAKE THE TRAIN, TOO! *SNIRFL!* I WANT TO GO HOME, TOO, WITH CORALIE!

COME ON NOW, MUNCHKIN...

I'M NOT A MUNCHKIN, *SIGH*!

I DON'T WANT TO GO TO YOUR NEW HOUSE, I DON'T WANT TO, I DON'T WANT TO, *SIGH*!

I WANT MOMMY, *SNIRFL*! I... I WANT YOU TWO TO GET BACK TOGETHER, *SIGH*!

HERE, BLOW YOUR NOSE, HONEY. AND SLEEP A LITTLE, YOU'RE TIRED.

THE SUN WILL RISE SOON...

WE'RE ALMOST THERE.

OUR STONES, THERE... DO THEY REALLY WALK, OR IS THAT JUST GROWN-UPS BEING DUMB?

OF COURSE THEY WALK, HAHA!

HELLO, I'M FLINT!

AND I'M LIMEROCK!

COOL!

GO FOR A WALK?

WOW...

LOOK, IT'S DOWN THERE, ON THE OTHER SIDE OF THE HILL...

IT'S BEAUTIFUL, ISN'T IT?

IT'S CALLED A "PENINSULA" BECAUSE IT'S AN ISLAND THAT'S CONNECTED TO THE MAINLAND ONLY BY A SMALL BRANCH OF EARTH...

AND YOUR SECOND HOUSE WILL BE HERE FROM NOW ON...

⇒KZZT⇐...
END OF THE LINE...
⇒KZZT⇐...

OUR COMPANY HOPES YOU'VE HAD A PLEASANT TRIP...

FINALLY HERE!

MY SWEET FREDDY!

I CAN'T WAIT TO SEE YOU AGAIN.

ARE YOU WAITING FOR SOMEONE, MISS?

I CAN DROP YOU OFF SOMEWHERE, IF YOU LIKE!

FREDDY!

I MISSED YOU SO MUCH! I STARTED IMAGINING SOMETHING AWFUL.

HUSH NOW...

I DON'T WANT TO EVER BE AWAY FROM YOU AGAIN.

IN A FEW MINUTES, THE TRAIN WILL ARRIVE AT THE FINAL STATION. PLEASE BE SURE TO NOT LEAVE ANYTHING BEHIND! ⇒KZZZT⇐...

HUH, WHAT?

⇒KZZZT⇐... HOPES YOU'VE HAD A PLEASANT TRIP...

DARN, I FELL ASLEEP.

FRE... FREDDY...

MAYBE I SHOULD HAVE TEXTED HIM TO LET HIM KNOW ABOUT MY ARRIVAL.

BEST TO SURPRISE HIM.

HEE HEE! CAN'T WAIT TO SEE THE LOOK ON HIS FACE!

WHAT'S WRONG MY LOVE? YOU HAVEN'T TOUCHED YOUR BREAKFAST.

IS SOMETH... WRONG

NO, NOTHIN... I JUST HAVE A B... FEELING...

REBECCA, WAKE UP!

WE'RE HERE!

QUICK, HURRY UP...

YOU'RE GOING TO MISS A MAGNIFICENT SUNRISE.

I DON'T CARE ABOUT THE SUN! I WANT TO SLEEP!

KIDS NEED THEIR SLEEP! IT'S GOOD FOR THEIR GROWTH!

...AND I WANT TO GROW BIGGER!

YOU'RE MISSING EVERYTHING.

ME ON NOW, ON'T BE SO RDHEADED!

YOU WON'T REGRET IT...

≷GRMBLLL≷...

LOOK...

WHAT DID I TELL YOU?

PFF≷... ON'T RE FOR RTERS... MBLL≷...

I WANT TO SLEEP... THE SUN IS STUPID AND...

WOW...

THIS IS THE LAND OF WALKING STONES!

WELL, WHAT DID I TELL YOU?

DO YOU LIKE IT?

IT'S INCREDIBLE!

IT'S LIKE A MAGIC KINGDOM IN FAIRY TALES!

THAT'S IT EXACTLY! IT'S A MAGIC KINGDOM!

YOUR KINGDOM...

AND YO ITS PRINC

REALLY?

OF COURSE! COME TAKE A CLOSER LOOK...

GIVE ME YOUR HAND, IT'S SLIPPERY.

LET'S GO GREET YOUR LOYAL SUBJECTS!

...THE WALKING STONES!

THE WALKING STONES?! THEY REALLY EXIST?!

SHH, YOU'LL W THEM UP...

- 14 -

Y'RE VERY [RF]UL, LITTLE [CR]EATURES...

WE MUSTN'T FRIGHTEN THEM.

LOOK, SWEETIE, THE WHOLE WORLD'S STILL ASLEEP...

THIS KINGDOM BELONGS TO YOU ALONE!

COOL!

GET YOUR NECK GOOD AND WET. THAT'S THE RULE FOR ENTERING THIS SECRET TERRITORY!

DONE!

[REA]DY, SWEET [PRI]NCESS?

READY!

PLOF

:BLB, BLB!:

:BLB?:

[I]S REALLY COLD, [H]A HA HA!

SO, DID YOU SEE THEM?

NO, IT WAS ALL BLURRY!

MY EYES STING, DADDY!

THAT'S NORMAL, HONEY. THE STONES THAT WALK SEED THE SEAWATER WITH SALT...

...TO KEEP FISHERMEN FROM CAPTURING THEM...

...TOMORROW, WE'LL GO TO BIG D'S STORE AND BUY YOU A DIVING MASK...

...SO YOU'LL BE ABLE TO SEE THEM...

- 15 -

YOU SEE THAT? WHAT WAS IT?

SOME KIND OF "LAND MONSTERS."

THE LITTLE ONE WITH THE PINK HAIR SEEMED SORTA NICE.

THEY'RE ALL RIGHT WHEN THEY'RE STILL YOUNG. THEY GET DANGEROUS ONCE THEY GROW UP!

THEY POLLUTE, THEY DESTROY EVERYTHING!

I THINK THEY'RE CALLED...

"HUMA

AND THE LITTLE GIRL WITH PINK HAIR IS UNDER MY PROTECTION.

SO, WATCH WHAT YOU SAY!

OKAY... SO I'LL SAY GOODBYE, HEH HEH...

MY GOODNESS. YOU LOOK KIND OF PALE FOR A SEA ANEMONE...

I'M A MICROBE.

A WHAT?

OH, ANOTHER UNLUCKY ONE INJURED BY A HOOK...

A MICROBE!

COME HERE, YOU...

DON'T BE AFRAID.

YEAH WELL... MICROBE OR NOT, WATCH OUT... HUMANS ARE MEAN. THEY WON'T HESITATE TO BETRAY YOU OR ABANDON YOU WHEN THEY NO LONGER NEED YOU!

BLOB BLOB

THE LITTLE HUMAN WITH PINK HAIR IS MY FRIEND...

SHE'D NEVER ABANDON ME...

BLOB BLOB

SHE JUST NEEDS TO SPEND A LITTLE T WITH HER DAD...

...THAT'S ALL!

CRICH CRICH

CRICH

REBEL

DADDY DOESN'T REALLY LIVE IN A HOUSE. IT'S A KIND OF A TRAILER, BUT BETTER: IT'S CALLED A "MOBILE HOME..."

INSIDE IT'S DELUXE! THERE'S MY BEDROOM, A BATHROOM, AND EVEN A KITCHEN... BUT SINCE IT'S HOT OUT, WE DO BARBECUES ON THE PATIO...

...DY BOUGHT A BIG FISH AT THE PORT THAT'S ...OCATED JUST BESIDE OUR CAMPGROUND...

THE LAND OF WALKING STONES ISN'T VERY BIG, BUT IT'S REALLY PRETTY. (I'LL TRY TO SHOW THAT WITH A DRAWING, BU IT ISN'T EASY...)

DURING THE SUMMER, THERE ARE LOTS OF FOLKS AT THE CAMPGROUND, AND FEWER PEOPLE IN THE WINTER... THE FOUR NEIGHBORS WHO LIVE THERE ALL YEAR ARE:

I DON'T KNOW THEM VERY WELL YET, BUT EVERYONE SEEMS TO GET ALONG GOOD... LIKE IN AN IDEAL FAMILY...

PUT AWAY YOUR COLORED PENCILS, REBECCA, IT'S TIME TO EAT!

THAT SMELLS REAL GOOD, ROBOT, BRAVO! YOU'RE AN EXCELLENT COOK!

THANKS, "CAPTAIN REBECCA"! MEEP! THE OMEGA 3 CONTAINED IN THIS FISH WILL ACCELERATE YOUR GROWTH! MEEP!

YEAAH!

DO YOU WANT A LITTLE SALAD, CAPTAIN? MEEP?

DO YOU WANT ME TO MAKE THE VINAIGRETTE, ROBOT?

DARN, I FORGOT TO BUY SOME OLIVE OIL!

COULD YOU GO ASK SABINE FOR SOME, PLEASE?

I'LL GO! GO AHEAD, TIME ME!

ONE... MEEP!

TWO... MEEP!

I'M GOING TO TRY TO BEAT MY RECORD!

...THREE... MEEP! FOUR...

SABINE, ARE YOU THERE?

I'M ON A MISSION!

I NEED SOME OLIVE OIL!

SABINE IT'S URGENT!

I'M BEING TIMED!

HI, RODRIGO, YOU STARTLED ME...

IS YOUR MOM HOME?

NO?!

ALL RIGHT, TOO BAD.

OKAY, I'M GONE...

LATER...

THANKS, RODRIGO, THAT'S NICE.

I'LL BRING IT BACK RIGHT AWAY!

YOU... WHAT ARE YOU DOING THERE?

I'M GOING FISHING.

WITH A SALAD BOWL AND AN OLD RAG?

YOU DON'T TALK MUCH, DO YOU?

IT'LL BE PERFECT HERE.

YOU PUT SOME ROCKS IN THE SALAD BOWL.

AND A LITTLE FLOUR.

YOU TAKE A RAG WITH A HOLE...

?

...AND YOU COVER THE BOWL USING A RUBBER BAND.

THEN YOU PUT IT IN THE WATER.

NOT TOO DEEP...

THIS KIND OF FISHING IS RESTRICTED TO NO MORE THAN ONCE IN A YEAR!

OTHERWISE, WE'D RUN OUT OF FISH!

'S THE RULES!

UNDERSTOOD?

ERSTOOD!

OKAY, NOW WE JUST GOT TO WAIT...

FUNNY KIND OF FISHING...

I WONDER IF MY DADDY KNOWS ABOUT IT...

...36, 322, MEEP...

...36, 323, MEEP...

...36, 324, MEEP...

HELLO, MOM... YES... BUT... MY TRAIN RAN LATE...

I KNOW, I SHOULD HAVE CALLED YOU...

YES...

WELL, NO...

THERE'S NO POINT COMING FOR ME AT THE STATION...

I'LL TAKE THIS OPPORTUNITY TO WALK AROUND TOWN BEFORE COMING HOME.

OKAY, SMOOCH.

MAY I HELP YOU, MISS?

I'LL TAKE THIS...

DO YOU WANT IT GIFT WRAPPED?

YES, PLEASE.

THIS T-SHIRT WILL FIT HIM LIKE A GLOVE...

CAN'T WAIT TO SEE HIS FACE WHEN HE SEES ME...

AND HIM, SO PROUD, HEE HEE...

I HOPE YOU LIKE SURPRISES AT LEAST, FREDDY STEVENS!

PEEKABOO! SO--

I... ...

TEXT ME, OR WE'LL CALL, OKAY?

OKAY, KISSES...

GLIC

YOU HAVE TO PUT YOUR HAND OVER THE HOLE TO KEEP THE FISH FROM GETTING AWAY!

WOW! THERE'S LOTS OF THEM!

N ALL KINDS COLORS! 'S A SUPER GE CATCH!

REMEMBER WELL: "DON'T DO THIS MORE THAN ONCE A YEAR," OTHERWISE...

"...OTHERWISE THERE WON'T BE ANY FISH LEFT!"

ALL RIGHT, I'M UNDERSTOOD. I'M NOT STUPID!

GOOD...

OKAY, LET'S SEE WHAT WE HAVE. THAT'S A SAR... A LITTLE MULLET...

..A SAND EENBRAS, BREAM, A...

BUT... WHAT'S THIS THING?!

I'VE NEVER SEEN A FISH WITH A HEAD LIKE THAT!

IT MUST BE RADIOACTIVE. I'D BETTER TO THROW IT BACK...

BUT... IT LOOKS LIKE...

ERNEST! THAT'S ERNEST! HE'S MY BEST FRIEND!

YOU'RE COMPLETELY CRAZY!

HE'S WAY NICE AND PER STRONG... HE'S A MICROBE!

AND YOU'VE "CAUGHT" HIM, HA HA!

AAAA--

CHOOO!

HELLO, LITTLE MICROBE!

LOOK, WHAT DID I TELL YOU?! DO YOU BELIEVE ME NOW?

=SNIFLE

BLOB BLOB

I'VE NEVER SEEN ANYTHING LIKE IT...

WHAT ARE YOU MADE OF? PLASTIC?

HE'S GOT LOTS OF SUPERPOWERS! GO ON, SHOW HIM, ERNEST!

TUP TUP

ARE YOU READY?

ATTENTION... DEMONSTRATION.

HM, HM...

MY NAME'S ERNEST!

I'M A SUPER MICROBE!

BLOB

THE STRONGEST ONE OF ALL!

BLOB

BLOB

I CAN TRANSFORM MYSELF...

MULTIPLY MYSELF...

BLOB

BLOB

IMITATE...

I DON'T LIKE YOUR FACE, YOU'RE WEIRD!

I CAN GRANT ALL YOUR WISHES!

BLOB

BLOB

IN SHORT...

...IN ONE WORD...

...I'M COOL!

BLOB

PUT 'ER THERE, BUDDY! WE'RE GOING TO GET ALONG GREAT!

SO, WHAT WISH DO YOU WANT GRANTED?

I'D LIKE YOU TO LEAVE ME ALONE!

AND DON'T TOUCH ME. I DON'T WANT TO BECOME RADIOACTIVE, GOT IT?

!

I'M NOT A BABY. I DON'T NEED A NANNY!

"I'M NOT A BABY, I DON'T NEED A NANNY"...

STOP THAT, IT'S NOT FUNNY!

DISAPPEAR.

SPLOSH

YOU DON'T SCARE ME WITH YOUR HOCUS-POCUS!

ARE YOU CERTAIN?

IT IS "SHARK WEEK"!

AOOOW!

YOUR "JAWS" IMITATION IS LAME.

TAC

OKAY, I'M GOING TO GO FISH FOR AN OCTOPUS FOR TONIGHT'S DINNER...

BLOB BLOB

ARE YOU OKAY, ERNEST?

AAAAH OKAY...

DON'T WORRY. I THINK RODRIGO ISN'T AS WILD AS HE SEEMS.

NAAH A PRO'LEM.

I'M HAPPY YOU CAME BACK, ERNEST.

WE HAVEN'T SEEN EACH OTHER IN A WHILE...

WHERE DID YOU GO?

I WAS 'ERE, 'UT 'OU 'ERE 'OO 'USY 'AYING 'ITH YOUR 'EW 'RIENDS 'O 'AY 'TTENTION TO 'E.

I DON'T UNDERSTAND YOU. TAKE THAT STICK OUT OF YOUR MOUTH!

I SAID: "I WAS THERE, BUT YOU WERE TOO BUSY PLAYING WITH YOUR NEW FRIENDS TO PAY ATTENTION TO ME."

YOU ONLY CALL ME WHEN YOU'RE BORED...

DON'T SAY THAT, ERNEST. YOU'RE BEING MEAN, AND IT'S HURTING ME.

BUT IT'S THE TRUTH!

LESS NOISE, PLEASE!

YOU'LL MAKE 'SWIM AWAY.

YOU FISH FOR OCTOPUS WITHOUT A POLE OR BOWL, RODRIGO?

NO NEED.

MY FIST IS ENOUGH! THOSE IDIOTS LIKE TO TWIST THEIR TENTACLES AROUND EVERYTHING CROSSING THEIR PATH...

THEN YOU JUST SCOOP 'EM UP...

THEY LIKE TO HIDE AMO THE ROCKS

HUP!

SPRK

YOW!

PI.

TOO BIG!

THEIR FLESH IS RUBBERY!

THAT ONE'LL DO THE JOB...

C'M'ERE, LITTLE GUY...

SO, WHAT DO YOU SAY ABOUT THAT?

IT'S DELICIOUS SLICED THIN IN A SALAD WITH GARLIC AND PARSLEY!

LET HIM GO, RODRIGO, HE'S TOO LITTLE.

SO WHAT?

SO, HE HAS A RIGHT TO GROW UP AND LIVE HIS LIFE JUST LIKE US!

AND HAVE YOU THOUGHT OF HIS PARENTS? THEY MUST BE WORRIED TO DEATH.

PI PI

OURS, TOO, FOR THAT MATTER... IT'S LATE, WE'RE GOING TO GET IN TROUBLE.

THERE!

SPLASH

BY THE WAY, I MEANT TO SPECIFY THAT I'M NOT "RADIOACTIVE."

... I SAW 'EM PASS BY THE PORT WITH A BOWL AND BIG PAIL OF WATER...

THEY MUSTN'T BE FAR AWAY...

BIG D, IT'S YOUR TURN!

I DON'T LIKE IT WHEN SHE DISAPPEARS WITH NO WARNING! THAT KID'S ALWAYS TOO HEADSTRONG!

DON'T YOU WORRY. RODRIGO KNOWS THE AREA.

E'LL TAKE ONE AST LOOK AT THE JETTY.

GOOD NIGHT.

RODRIIIGO!

REBEEEECAAAA!

RODRIIIIGO!

HOW'S IT GOING WITH REBECCA'S MOM?

IT'S ALL RIGHT.

S NOT EASY ON THE GIRLS ESPECIALLY.

THE OLDER ONE, CORALIE, IS HAVING A TEENAGE CRISIS...

REBECCAAA!

OKAY, COME SIT DOWN AND RELAX A LITTLE.

THEY MUST BE BACK AT THE CAMPGROUND WAITING FOR US.

YOU LOOK KINDA CUTE, YOU KNOW?

ND YOU?

WITH RODRIGO'S DAD?

HMM...

I LIKE BEING WITH YOU...

I FIXED YOU A SANDWICH, HONEY.

ARE YOU SURE YOU'RE NOT HUNGRY?

LEAVE ME ALONE, MOM, GO AWAY!

WELL?

NOT GOOD.

I THINK IT'S HER BOYFRIEND...

YOU SHOULDN'T LET HER TALK TO YOU WITH THAT TONE.

YOU WANT ME TO TALK TO HER?

UH, NO THANKS. STAY OUT OF IT, PLEASE...

I HATE YOU ALL!

DING DONG

WHO'S RINGING THE BELL AT THIS HOUR?

YES, ONE MOMENT!

UH... IT'S FOR YOU, HONEY...

WELL, MISS SECRETIVE? WHY DIDN'T YOU TELL ME YOU WERE BACK?

...ERE DID YOU TWO GO? WE WERE WORRIED SICK!

HAVE YOU SEEN THE TIME?

I DON'T WANT YOU HEADING OFF LIKE THAT WITHOUT TELLING ME!

WHAT DID YOU DO ALL THAT TIME?

WE WERE FISHING WITH A BOWL.

...ECCA...?

IT'S THE TRUTH! IT'S A FISHING SECRET AND YOU WON'T EVER KNOW A THING BECAUSE YOU'RE TOO GROUCHY!

SO THERE!

...AND THEN ERNEST APPEARED. SO I INTRODUCED HIM TO RODRIGO...

...AND THEN WE FREED AN OCTOPUS...

...AND THEN... AND THEN...

SO? HAVE YOU FOUND OUR LITTLE FUGITIVES?

...BIG D! NICOLE! COME IN, WE'RE HAVING COCKTAILS!

...WON'T ...AY NO...

COCKTAILS? AT 10 PM?

RELAX, BUDDY...

YOU'RE ON VACATION...

OOOH, NICE FISH!

WE'LL HAVE A NICE FISHFRY!

RELAX, BUDDY...

YOU'RE ON VACATION...

CAN I HELP YOU FRY THE FISH, NICOLE?

YES, REBECCA, BUT BE CAREFUL TO NOT BURN YOURSELF!

COME ON, DON'T STAY THERE... YOU DRINKING SOMETHING?

UH... SAME AS YOU.

WHO'S "ERNEST"?

NO IDEA...

- 27 -

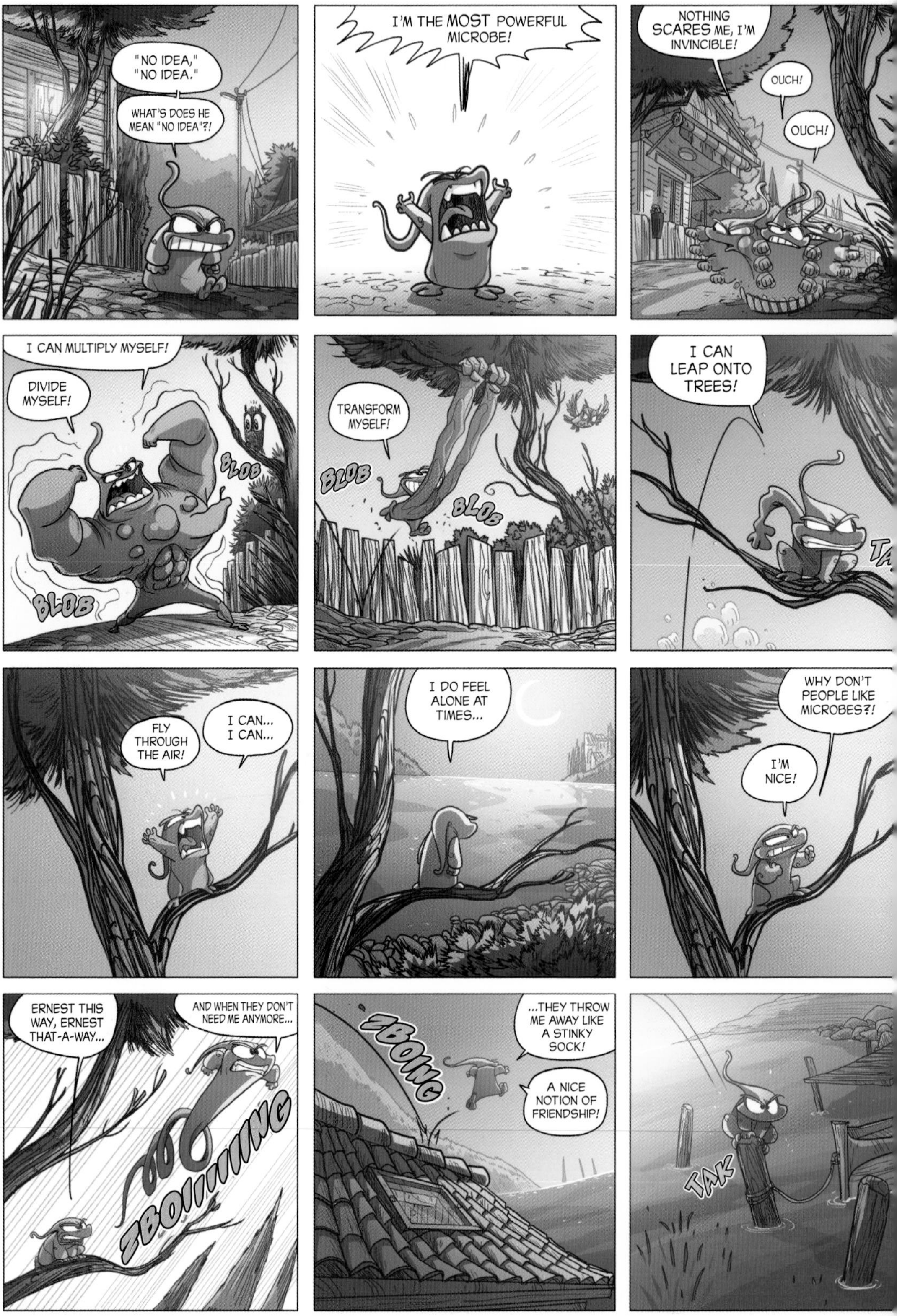
"NO IDEA,"
"NO IDEA."
WHAT'S DOES HE MEAN "NO IDEA"?!
I'M THE MOST POWERFUL MICROBE!
NOTHING SCARES ME, I'M INVINCIBLE!
OUCH!
OUCH!
I CAN MULTIPLY MYSELF!
DIVIDE MYSELF!
BLOB
BLOB
TRANSFORM MYSELF!
BLOB
BLOB
I CAN LEAP ONTO TREES!
I CAN... I CAN...
FLY THROUGH THE AIR!
I DO FEEL ALONE AT TIMES...
WHY DON'T PEOPLE LIKE MICROBES?!
I'M NICE!
ERNEST THIS WAY, ERNEST THAT-A-WAY...
AND WHEN THEY DON'T NEED ME ANYMORE...
ZBOIIIIIIING
ZBOING
...THEY THROW ME AWAY LIKE A STINKY SOCK!
A NICE NOTION OF FRIENDSHIP!
TAK

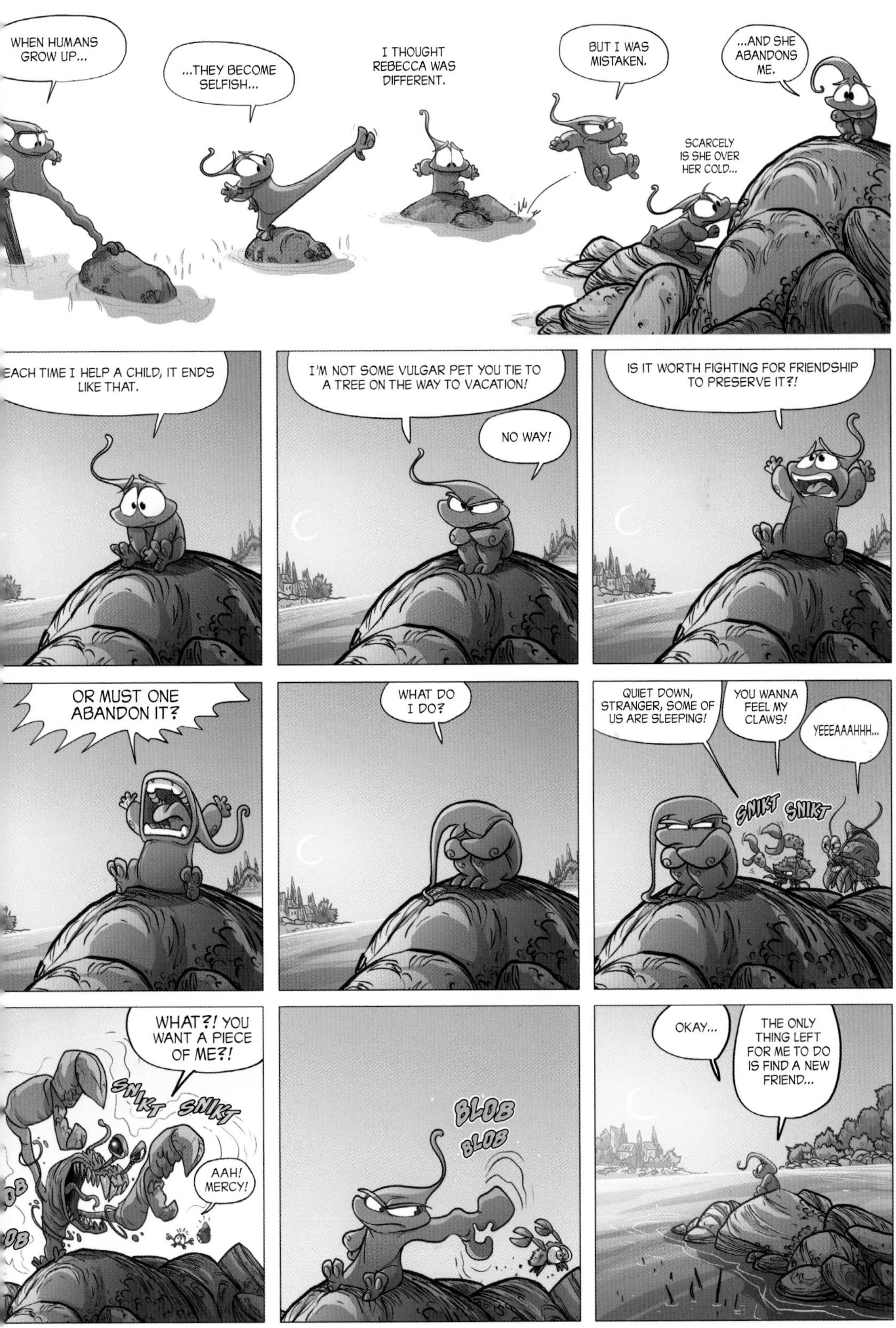

WHEN HUMANS GROW UP...
...THEY BECOME SELFISH...
I THOUGHT REBECCA WAS DIFFERENT.
BUT I WAS MISTAKEN.
SCARCELY IS SHE OVER HER COLD...
...AND SHE ABANDONS ME.
EACH TIME I HELP A CHILD, IT ENDS LIKE THAT.
I'M NOT SOME VULGAR PET YOU TIE TO A TREE ON THE WAY TO VACATION!
NO WAY!
IS IT WORTH FIGHTING FOR FRIENDSHIP TO PRESERVE IT?!
OR MUST ONE ABANDON IT?
WHAT DO I DO?
QUIET DOWN, STRANGER, SOME OF US ARE SLEEPING!
YOU WANNA FEEL MY CLAWS!
YEEEAAAHHH...
SNIKT SNIKT
WHAT?! YOU WANT A PIECE OF ME?!
SNIKT SNIKT
AAH! MERCY!
BLOB BLOB
OKAY...
THE ONLY THING LEFT FOR ME TO DO IS FIND A NEW FRIEND...

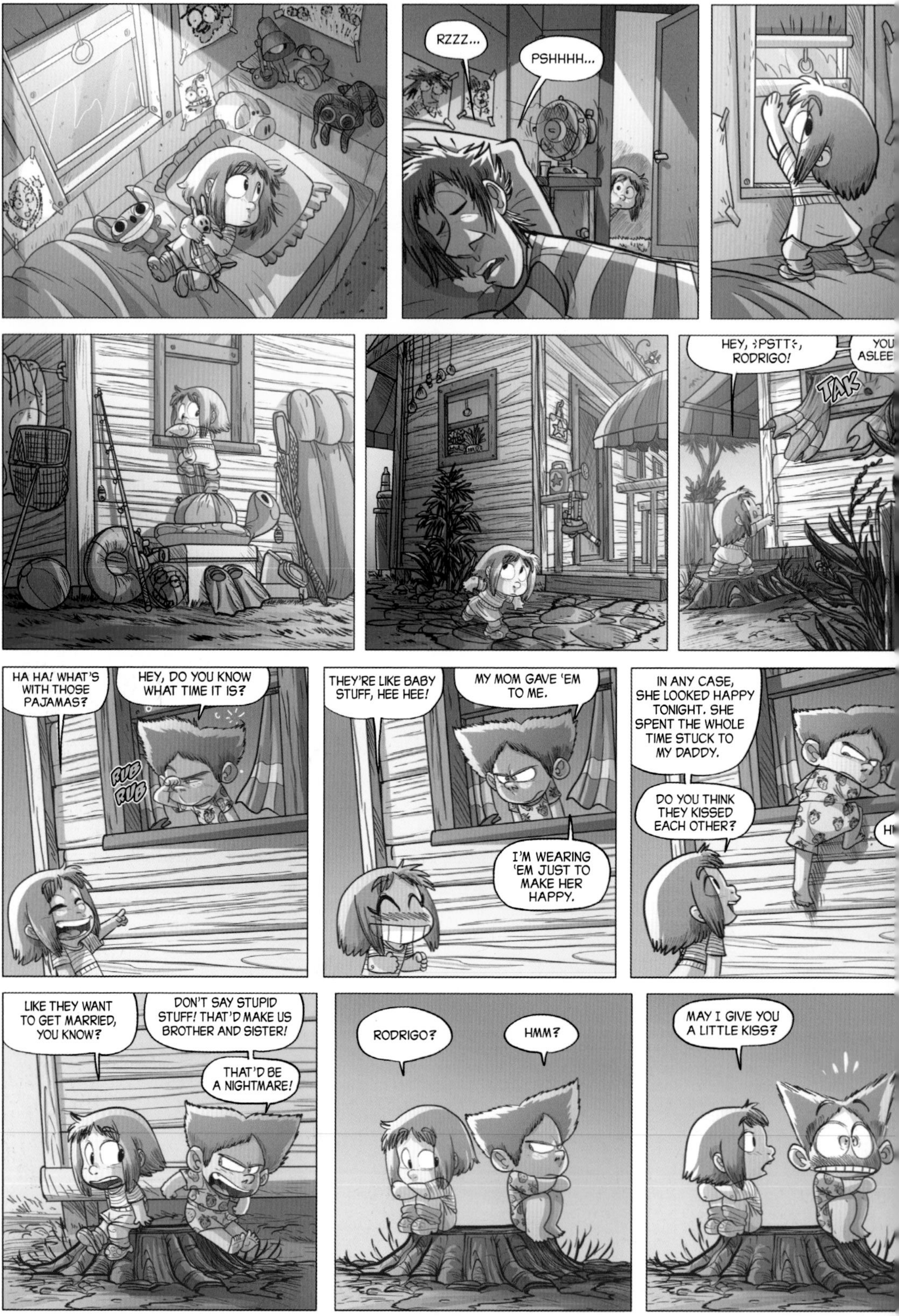
RZZZ...
PSHHHH...
HEY, ⁑PSTT⁑, RODRIGO!
YOU ASLEE
TAK
HA HA! WHAT'S WITH THOSE PAJAMAS?
HEY, DO YOU KNOW WHAT TIME IT IS?
RUB RUB
THEY'RE LIKE BABY STUFF, HEE HEE!
MY MOM GAVE 'EM TO ME.
I'M WEARING 'EM JUST TO MAKE HER HAPPY.
IN ANY CASE, SHE LOOKED HAPPY TONIGHT. SHE SPENT THE WHOLE TIME STUCK TO MY DADDY.
DO YOU THINK THEY KISSED EACH OTHER?
LIKE THEY WANT TO GET MARRIED, YOU KNOW?
DON'T SAY STUPID STUFF! THAT'D MAKE US BROTHER AND SISTER!
THAT'D BE A NIGHTMARE!
RODRIGO?
HMM?
MAY I GIVE YOU A LITTLE KISS?

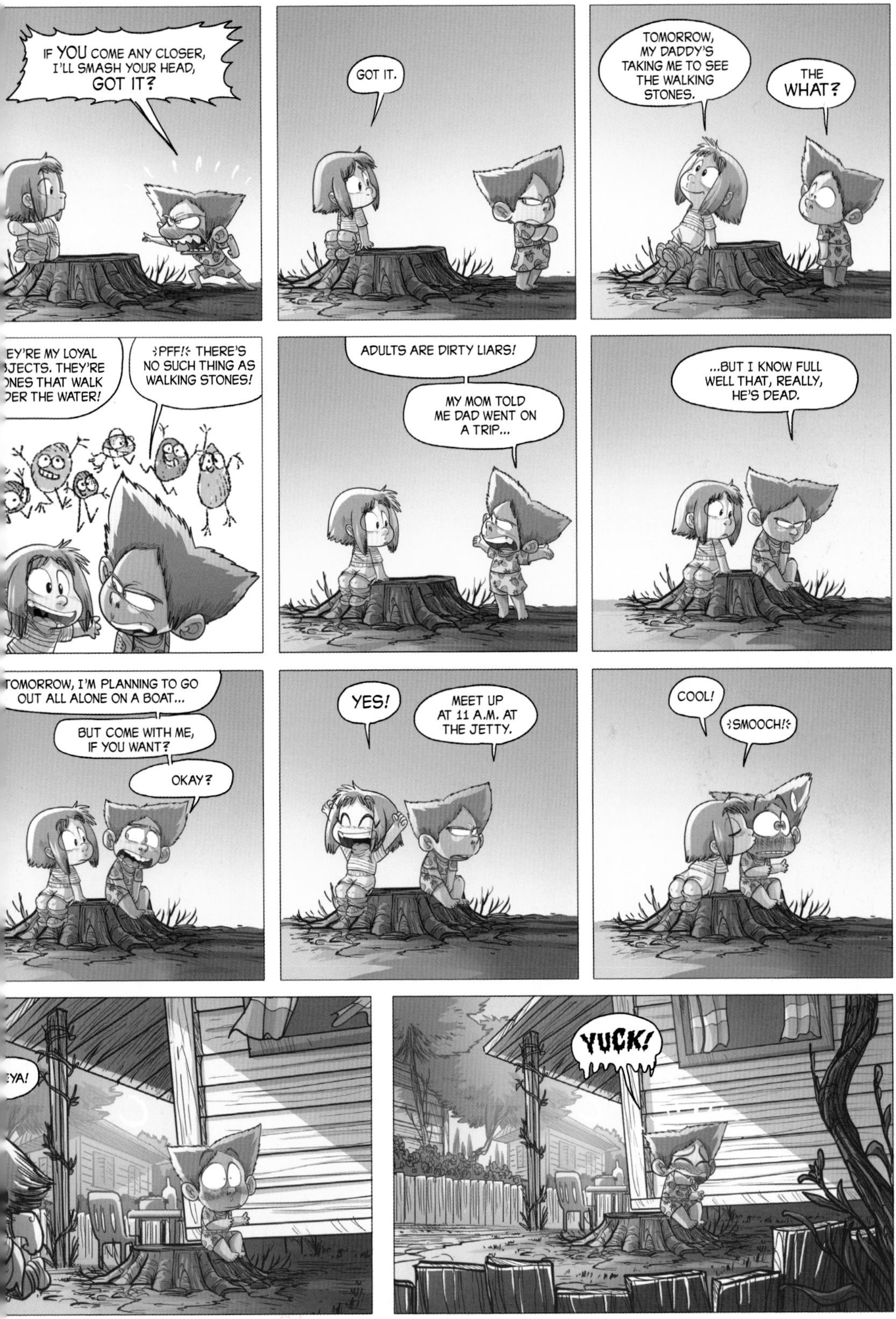
IF YOU COME ANY CLOSER, I'LL SMASH YOUR HEAD, GOT IT?
GOT IT.
TOMORROW, MY DADDY'S TAKING ME TO SEE THE WALKING STONES.
THE WHAT?
EY'RE MY LOYAL BJECTS. THEY'RE ONES THAT WALK DER THE WATER!
PFF! THERE'S NO SUCH THING AS WALKING STONES!
ADULTS ARE DIRTY LIARS!
MY MOM TOLD ME DAD WENT ON A TRIP...
...BUT I KNOW FULL WELL THAT, REALLY, HE'S DEAD.
TOMORROW, I'M PLANNING TO GO OUT ALL ALONE ON A BOAT...
BUT COME WITH ME, IF YOU WANT?
OKAY?
YES!
MEET UP AT 11 A.M. AT THE JETTY.
COOL!
SMOOCH!
YA!
YUCK!

FREDDY, I... HOW CAN I PUT IT?

YOU...

...DO YOU REALLY HAVE FEELINGS FOR ME?

YES, YOU CLAIM, BUT YOU'RE LYING...

I SAW YOU YESTERDAY, WITH JESSICA!

I S... YOU K... HE...

YOU'VE BROKEN MY HEART, FREDDY! WHY?!

I TRUSTED YOU...SNIRF!

YOU'LL REGRET THE DAY YOU WERE BORN, FREDDY STEVENS! I GUARANTEE YOU THAT!

...ARE YOU OKAY, HONEY?

YOUR FRIEND'S WAITING OUTSIDE AND... UH... IT'S LATE...

...DO YOU WANT ME TO ASK HIM TO LEAVE?

THERE'S NO USE!

CORALIE, I THINK YOU'D DO BETTER TO...

AH! I WAS GETTING READY TO LEAVE... UH... HOW ARE YOU?

SHUT UP!

I LEFT THE TEA ON THE STOVE...

OKAY THEN, HEH HEH...

I'M GOING...

I LOVE YOU, FREDDY... I'LL CALL YOU TOMORROW!

WOW... MY GOODNESS... WHEW...

GOODNIGHT, CORALIE...

WOW...

JUST YOU WAIT, FREDDY STEVENS!

MY M...

WHAT'S RODRIGO UP TO?

MY FROG WATCH IS ALWAYS ON TIME.

AND HE'S LATE.

RDRIIIGO!

WHERE ARE YOU?!

RODRIIIGO!

WHAT'S THE MATTER, ONEY? WHY ARE YOU HERE ALL BY YOURSELF?

SABINE, I... I...

HAVE YOU SEEN RODRIGO?

RODRIGO?

HE LEFT WITH HIS BOAT THIS MORNING...

VERY EARLY...

WHAT?! DID I SAY SOMETHING I SHOULDN'T HAVE?

SURPRISE! LOOK WHAT I BOUGHT YOU, MUNCHKIN!

OKAY, LET'S GO TO THE LAND OF THE WALKING STONES.

I'M *NOT A MUNCHKIN!* AND YOU'RE *NOTHING BUT A DIRTY LIAR!*

UH... WHAT?!

WHAT... WHAT DID I SAY?

SO, DO YOU HEAR ME?

THE RECEPTION'S NOT GOOD... HELLO?

OH, YES, THAT'S BETTER!

SO, I WAS SAYING IT'S BEEN A WEEK...

...A WHOLE WEEK RODRIGO SEEMS TO BE AVOIDING ME...

WHENEVER I GO KNOCK ON HIS WINDOW, HIS MOM TELLS ME HE'S RESTING.

HE NEVER WANTS TO TAKE ME FISHING ON HIS BOAT. HE SAYS IT'S JUST TOO DANGEROUS.

I FEEL LONELY... SAD AND LONELY.

AND... AND ERNEST?

OH, I HAVEN'T SEEN HIM SINCE WE WENT FISHING WITH THE SALAD BOWL, BUT I DON'T CARE.

HE CAN STAY WHEREVER HE IS, THAT DIRTY GERM...

I MISS YOU BOTH...

LOTS AND LOTS...

I... I KNOW A SONG THAT COULD HELP YOU, SWEETHEART...

...A MAGIC SONG...

REALLY?

GO AHEAD, SING IT FOR ME!

PLEASE PLEASE PLEAS

"...REPEAT ...ER ME..." | "ALL TROUBLES AND WORRIES..."

ALL TROUBLES AND WORRIES..."

"...ARE STINKY LIKE PEE!"

HA! HA! HA!

"...ARE STINKY LIKE PEE!"

GOOD. "BUT TO GET RID OF THEM..."

"BUT TO GET RID OF THEM..."

...NE SAY POOPY-FLEA!"

;PRFT...;

"WE SAY POOPY-FLEA!"

HA! HA! HA!

THANKS, I FEEL A LOT BETTER! YOUR MAGIC SONG REALLY WORKS...

YOU'RE NOT A LIAR.

I LOVE YOU SO, SO MUCH...

...LK TO YOU ...ON, GRANDPA BUG...*

TALK TO YOU SOON, SWEETHEART...

GOODNESS ME, YOU OLD COOT! WHAT'S GOT YOU SINGING SUCH SILLY RUBBISH?!

ARE YOU DRINKING AGAIN?

NO... UH... IT WAS THE KID...

I THINK SHE'S ALREADY MISSING THE COUNTRY AIR.

AND I MISS HER, TOO.

...R, LITTLE GIRL.

THE RELATIONSHIP BETWEEN HER PARENTS ISN'T EASY ON HER.

OKAY, COME SIT DOWN AT THE TABLE, IT'S READY.

COMING.

"WE SAY POOPY-FLEA!"

...NEST & REBECCA #3 "GRANDPA BUG."

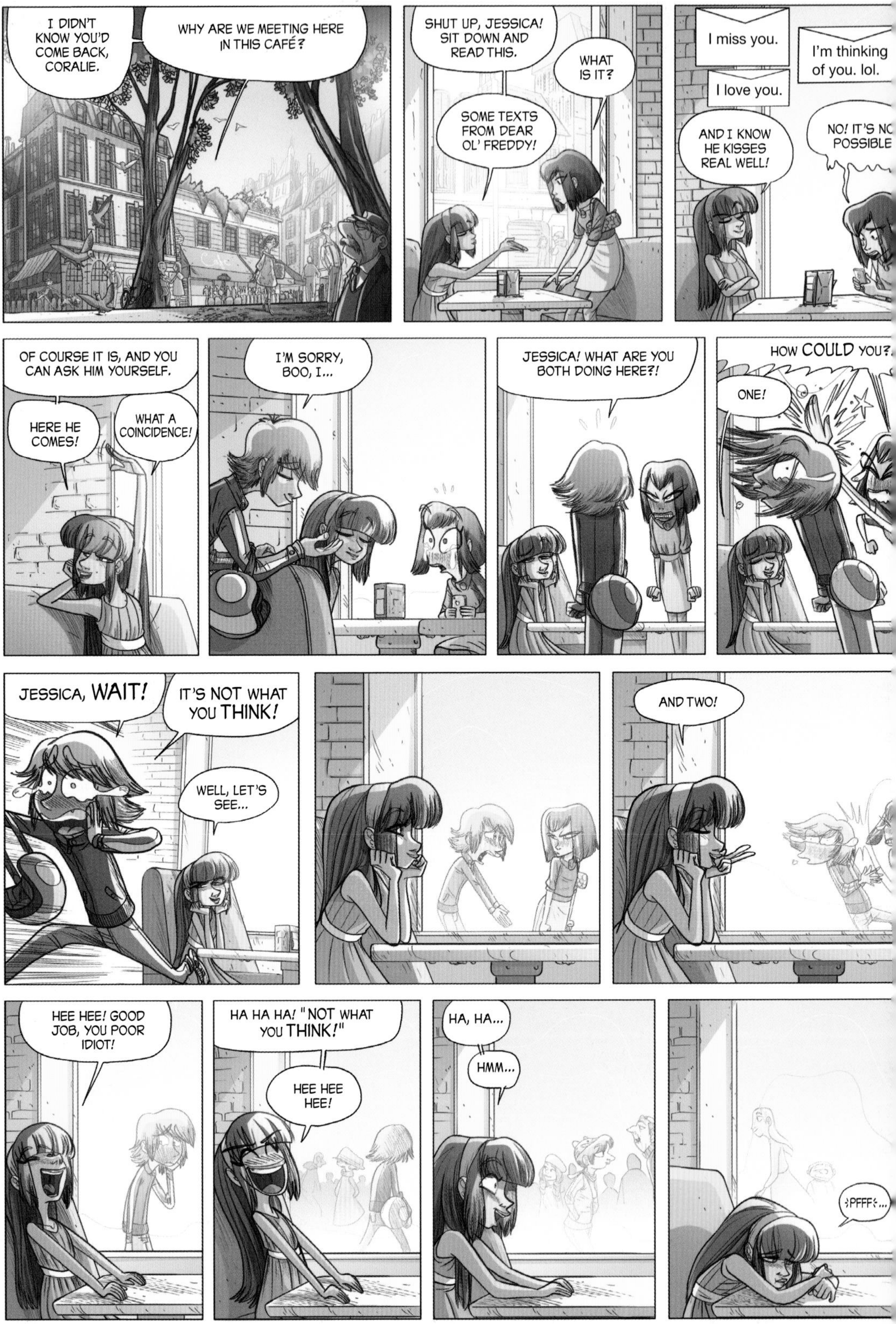
I DIDN'T KNOW YOU'D COME BACK, CORALIE.
WHY ARE WE MEETING HERE IN THIS CAFÉ?
SHUT UP, JESSICA! SIT DOWN AND READ THIS.
WHAT IS IT?
SOME TEXTS FROM DEAR OL' FREDDY!
I miss you.
I love you.
I'm thinking of you. lol.
AND I KNOW HE KISSES REAL WELL!
NO! IT'S NO POSSIBLE
OF COURSE IT IS, AND YOU CAN ASK HIM YOURSELF.
HERE HE COMES!
WHAT A COINCIDENCE!
I'M SORRY, BOO, I...
JESSICA! WHAT ARE YOU BOTH DOING HERE?!
HOW COULD YOU?
ONE!
JESSICA, WAIT!
IT'S NOT WHAT YOU THINK!
WELL, LET'S SEE...
AND TWO!
HEE HEE! GOOD JOB, YOU POOR IDIOT!
HA HA HA! "NOT WHAT YOU THINK!"
HEE HEE HEE!
HA, HA...
HMM...
PFFF...

...ME SEEMS TO DRAG OUT AND BE
LONGER WHEN YOU'RE BORED...

TO OCCUPY MYSELF A LITTLE, I DECIDED
TO PICK UP THE POLLUTION THAT'S
IN THE WATER...

...IT'S A LOT
OF WORK!

DADDY SAYS THAT'S WHY THE WALKING
STONES ARE BECOMING RARE...

ADULTS ARE
REALLY
STUPID...

...FEW DAYS, I'LL GO HOME TO MOMMY. I'LL BE HAPPY TO SEE
HER AND GET MY BEDROOM BACK, BUT...

...I'LL BE BORED WITHOUT
FRIENDS.

I HOPE ERNEST IS FINE AND THAT
HE DIDN'T GET CAPTURED BY
DR. FAKBERT.*

...IKE TO HAVE A FRIEND TO PLAY WITH,
FRIEND WHO TAKES CARE OF ME...

...BUT WISHES ONLY COME TRUE
IN MOVIES...

...IF YOU THINK REAL
D ABOUT THEM...

...REALLY,
REALLY
HARD...

WOOF!

MISSILE!**
IT'S YOU?!

IT'S REALLY
YOU?!

YOU FOUND
ME?!

...OUR PAWS ARE
ALL HURT!

...UT YOU
CAME...

WOOF!

...HANKS,
...ISSILE.

...KS.

SINCE
MISSILE CAME ALL
THIS WAY FOR ME,
GRANDPA BUG
SAID I COULD
KEEP HIM.

DOGS ARE BRAVE,
LOYAL BEINGS...

NOT LIKE MICROBES.

*ERNEST & REBECCA #1 AND #2.
**ERNEST & REBECCA #3.

TO BE ABLE TO SEE THE OCEAN DEPTHS, YOU NEED:

A PAIR OF FLIPPERS...

A MASK...

A SNORKEL...

...AND A LITTLE SKILL, OF COURSE!

SO, WE'L START B GETTING FEET WET

...IN ORDER TO PUT THE FLIPPERS ON CORRECTLY.

⁺UGH⁺ IT'S HARD!

IT'S EASIER TO GET INTO THE WATER BY BACKING UP.

LOOK! I'M A FROG: CROAK, CROAK!

NEXT YOU SPIT INSIDE YOUR M WHILE RUBBING IT GOOD W YOUR SALIVA!

YUCK THAT GROS

DO WE REALLY HAVE TO

YES, IT REMOVES THE CONDENSATION.

LIKE THIS...

SPUT

THAT'S GOOD, HONEY... BUT DON'T SPIT TOO MUCH.

AND THEN WE RINSE IT.

⁺SPIT!⁺

⁺SPIT!⁺

STICK YOUR MASK ON TIGHT BY LIFTING YOUR HAIR SO THE WATER DOESN'T GET IN.

⁺ARGH! I 'AN'T 'REATHE

YOU BREATHE THROUGH YOUR MOUTH, LIKE WHEN YOU HAVE A COLD.

BLOW OUT THROUGH YOUR SNORKEL TO MAKE SURE IT'S EMPTY.

THERE.

NOW YOU JUST HAVE TO SHAKE YOUR FROG LEGS AND FOLLOW ME...

READY?

READY!

SPLASH

SP

BLUB BLUB BLUB

¿GLURGL!¿

HA HA! LOOKS LIKE U SWALLOWED MOUTHFUL!

DON'T WORRY, IT HAPPENS EVEN TO THE BEST!

¿KOF!¿
¿KOF!¿

IT STINGS! ¿KOF!¿

ARE YOU ALL RIGHT, HONEY?

MY SNORKEL DOESN'T WORK! I ALMOST DROWNED!

THAT'S NORMAL. YOU FILLED IT WITH WATER WHILE DIVING!

YOU HAVE TO KEEP THE END OUT... LIKE THIS...

OU WANT TO GO DEEPER, HOLD YOUR BREATH...

F YOU BREATHE OUT REAL RD TO EXPEL THE WATER WHEN YOU COME UP...

WATCH... I'LL DEMONSTRATE...

BLUB BLUB BLUB

SAY, DADDY?

HMM?

YOU LOVE SABINE N LIKE YOU USED LOVE MOMMY?

¿GLURGL!¿

¿BUURGL¿ ¿KOF! ¿KOF!¿

¿KOF!¿

IT LOOKS LIKE YOU SWALLOWED A MOUTHFUL...!

DON'T WORRY... IT HAPPENS EVEN TO THE BEST...

¿KOF!¿
¿KOF!¿

HEY, YOU! GIVE ME THAT BACK!

;GULP!

REBECCA, DON'T GO TOO FAR!

PUFF PUFF

DIRTY, LITTLE THIEF!

COME OUT!

HEE HEE! YOU'RE FUNNY!

PLASH PLOSH

WHAT KIND OF ANIMAL ARE YOU?

WOOOOW.

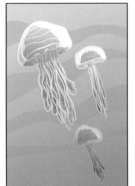

;PFLLOTCH!;

HA! HA!
HA! HEE!
HEE!

?

OWW!

SURRENDER!

NEVER!

SHOW YOURSELF!

YOU'LL PAY, BANDIT!

HA! HA!

YOU'RE TREMBLING, IS THAT IT...?

....YOU'RE TOO AFRAID OF "ONE-EYED RODRIGO"?!

YOU'RE AN EMBARRASSMENT TO PIRACY!

⸝YAAAAH!⸜

THERE YOU ARE AT LAST!

"ERNEST THE SWINDLER!"

SWINDLER YOURSELF!

KLING KLING

SPLOOSH

KLING KLING

SO, DO YOU SURRENDER?

THAT'S GOOD, ERNE YOU WIN, HEE HEE.

KLING

YOU REALLY ARE A SUPER MICROBE, OLD FRIEND!

HA! HA! HA!

I HATE YOU BOTH!

WHO WAS THAT?

REBECCA?

OH, NO...

- 42 -

EST AND RODRIGO
AME FRIENDS, AND
AT'S MORE, IT'S
HANKS TO ME!

THEY CUT ME OUT!

WHY DID THEY DO THAT TO ME?

BECAUSE I'M A GIRL?!

I'LL GET SUPER BIG, AND THEY'LL PAY FOR THAT!

SBAM

H, HONEY, ARE YOU OKAY?

YOU... YOU'RE CRYING?

MOMMY!

WE JUST GOT HERE...

WE WERE LOOKING EVERYWHERE FOR YOU!

MOMMY...

SAM AND MOMMY HAD DRIVEN ALL NIGHT COME GET ME, BRINGING WITH THEM THE END OF SUMMER...

DADDY AND SAM SHOOK HANDS REALLY HARD WHILE LOOKING AT EACH OTHER REAL WEIRD...

HEY!

HELLO!

MOMMY AND SABINE MET EACH OTHER...

A BEER?

NO ALCOHOL EVER, THANKS...

HEN WE HAD OCKTAIL WITH BIG D AND NICOLE...

WHEN ARE WE GOING HOME, MOMMY?

TOMORROW, SWEETIE... WE'RE GOING HOME TOMORROW.

WHAT?! VACATION'S ALREADY OVER?!

BUT... BUT WHAT ABOUT THE WALKING STONES?

...DADDY KEPT HIS WORD... JUST BEFORE WE LEFT, HE FINALLY SHOWED THEM TO ME...

...THE WALKING STONES REALLY DO EXIST...

MY DADDY ISN'T A LIAR...

THEY'RE ALSO CALLED "HERMIT CRABS..."

FLUB

FLUB

FLUB

HA HA! LOOK AT ALL THAT I GATHERED!

THEY'RE SO BEAUTIFUL! THEIR COLORS ARE WONDERFUL!

I'M GOING TO TAKE THEM HOME WITH ME! THAT WAY I'LL NEVER BE ALONE AGAIN!

ARE YOU SURE THAT'S A GOOD IDEA, HONEY?

DO YOU THINK THE[Y]'[LL] BE HAPP[Y] IN AN AQUARIUM...

YOU'RE RIGHT, DADDY...

I'M LUCKY: I'LL HAVE TWO HO[MES] FROM NOW ON...

THEY ONLY HAVE ONE...

...AND [I] HERE...

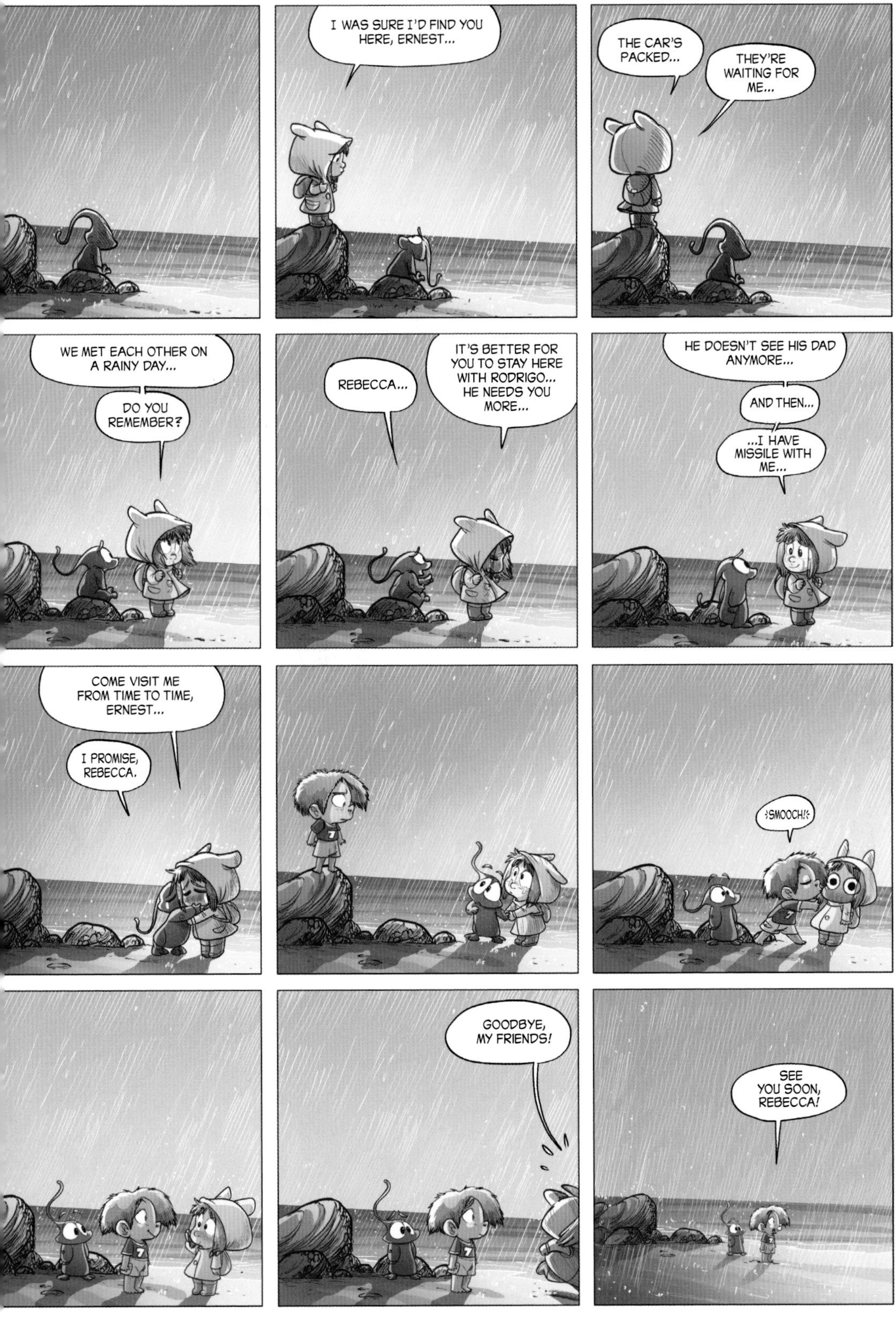
I WAS SURE I'D FIND YOU HERE, ERNEST...
THE CAR'S PACKED...
THEY'RE WAITING FOR ME...
WE MET EACH OTHER ON A RAINY DAY...
DO YOU REMEMBER?
REBECCA...
IT'S BETTER FOR YOU TO STAY HERE WITH RODRIGO... HE NEEDS YOU MORE...
HE DOESN'T SEE HIS DAD ANYMORE...
AND THEN...
...I HAVE MISSILE WITH ME...
COME VISIT ME FROM TIME TO TIME, ERNEST...
I PROMISE, REBECCA.
SMOOCH!
GOODBYE, MY FRIENDS!
SEE YOU SOON, REBECCA!

ON THE WAY BACK, I ALMOST DIDN'T GET SICK. I ONLY THREW UP FIVE TIMES...

MISSILE KEPT MY MORALE UP, AND HIS SNUGGLING DID ME GOOD.

THEN WE ARRIVED HOME... NOTHING MUCH HAS CHANGED HERE...

ONLY WHILE COMING IN, IT SEEMED TO ME LIKE THE HOUSE WAS EMPTIER AND COLDER THAN BEFORE...

ON THE OTHER HAND, CORALIE'S STILL LOCKED IN HER ROOM AND DOESN'T WANT TO SEE ANYONE.

DO NOT DISTURB

BY THE WAY, DIDN'T I TELL YOU? TOMORROW'S THE BIG DAY FOR ME...

OKAY, IT'S TIM[E] HONE[Y]

BACK-TO SCHOO[L] TOMORRO[W]

I'M GOING BACK TO SCHOOL!

AND I HAVE TO BE IN TOP FORM!

WE'LL PUT AWAY THE DRAWINGS AND IT'S BEDDY-BYE!

MOMMY? DO YOU THINK I'LL MAKE SOME FRIENDS THERE?

I DON'T DOUBT IT ONE SECOND, SWEETIE.

SLEEP TIGHT.

SMOOCH.

I LOVE YOU, MOMMY...

I LOVE YOU, TOO, HONEY...

SWEET DREAMS.

WATCH OUT FOR PAPERCUT Z ™

elcome to the fourth, family-centric ERNEST & REBECCA graphic novel from Papercutz, that microbe-
ed company dedicated to publishing great graphic novels for all ages. I'm Jim Salicrup, your
poallergenic Editor-in-Chief and recent holiday traveler. Believe it or not, whenever I tell folks that
percutz is proud to publish graphic novels for all ages, many tend to think that "all ages" means just
kids. And while admittedly, some Papercutz titles may appeal more to younger audiences than others,
NEST & REBECCA is my favorite example of a graphic novel series that truly appeals to all ages. With
liant writing by Guillaume Bianco, and stunning artwork by Antonello Dalena, we believe that ERNEST
REBECCA is one of the best graphic novel series being published today—for any age. Whether you're
t six and a half years old or as old as Grandpa Bug, we think you'll love ERNEST & REBECCA as much as
do!

ken together, ERNEST & REBECCA #3 "Grandpa Bug" and #4 "The Land of Walking Stones," tell the
e of an emotionally eventful family vacation. Having just taken such a vacation myself, I feel as if I just
ed through these stories. Well, maybe I didn't experience quite the emotional roller coaster ride that
becca did, but even the quiet moments really resonated with me. Like when I spent a few nights at my
ughter's grandfather's old farmhouse, I know exactly how this feels:

OUTSIDE, NO NOISE, NO CARS, NOTHING...

...JUST A STUPID, OLD ROOSTER THAT CROWS THREE TIMES AN HOUR...

Or when Rodrigo goes fishing for octopus, that reminds me
of my trip to Spain a few years ago, at a wonderful Comics
Festival in Granada, when all the guests and attendees were
treated to a special octopus dinner…

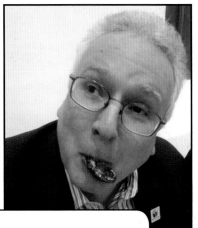

nsidering what an amazing job Bianco and Dalena did in
oturing the sense memories of a family vacation, I shudder
how well they may recreate the experience of going back
school, which we'll all see in ERNEST & REBECCA #5 "The
hool of Silliness." If anyone can make me look forward to re-
ng (through Rebecca) my early school days, it's the creators
ERNEST & REBECCA! I just don't want to do it alone, so I hope
u'll be there with me!

Thanks,

JIM

STAY IN TOUCH!

EMAIL: salicrup@papercutz.com
WEB: www.papercutz.com
TWITTER: @papercutzgn
FACEBOOK: PAPERCUTZGRAPHICNOVELS
FAN MAIL: Papercutz, 160 Broadway, Suite 700, East Wing,
            New York, NY 10038

SEE ERNEST AND REBECCA AGAIN
VERY SOON IN VOLUME FIVE, TITLED:
"THE SCHOOL OF SILLINESS."